34

For Matt! :)
Enjoy the
silliness
Kara Bartley

34

11 Short Stories

KARA BARTLEY

Library of Congress Control Number: 2013906280

ISBN:	Hardcover	978-1-4836-2022-0
	Softcover	978-1-4836-2021-3
	Ebook	978-1-4836-2023-7

This book was printed in the United States of America.

Rev. date: 04/05/2013

To order additional copies of this book, contact:
Xlibris Corporation
1-888-795-4274
www.Xlibris.com
Orders@Xlibris.com
131798

CONTENTS

For Bianca, who gave this book wings to fly.
Although we are separated by time,
Your essence is strong in those who love you

ONE

MY PAL, JAWS

He started out the size of a plum, although he was more like a deflated prune. Okay, that's a bad example. He was squished, flat, like a piece of processed cheese, yeah—that's more like it. He was cute and silver and adorable. Well, as adorable as a fish can be, I suppose. When I first spotted him in the pet shop, I was immediately drawn to him. From the side, he looked like a triangle with spaghetti hanging from his points. He was perched beside a dancing skeleton that was missing its upper torso. The bony legs moved about in the water as one remained tethered to a jewelled treasure chest.

"That's an angelfish," the shopkeeper said as he walked by.

"He's cute," I said.

The man just looked at me with a weird expression, as if I had told a bad joke. "You want him? He's yours!"

"*What*? What do you mean?"

"I mean . . . he's all yours. Free. Please take him!" The man look scared, yet he was smiling in an extremely insincere way.

I laughed and then said nothing as I stared at him. "You want to give me a fish for free?"

"Yes," he said.

I wasn't sure if he was joking or not. But there wasn't any response time because he was already headed for the tank.

"Wait a minute," I followed. "I just came in to get some cat toys."

"Doesn't matter," he said. "He's yours now." The man seemed frantic; desperate to expel the little animal from his store. He dropped a net into the tank and the angelfish swam into it, willingly. That should have been my first indication that something was off.

The man then pulled out the net and dropped the fish into a large, clear bag filled with water. He tied a knot around the top and placed the bag into my hand. He then withdrew a tiny square container from his pocket and placed it in my other hand. "That's his food," he pointed. "Don't worry—you won't need much."

I still couldn't believe what was happening.

"Thanks for stopping by," he said, ushering me out of the store.

The door locked behind me before I had a chance to breathe.

"But what about my cat toys . . ." I yelled on the other side of the glass. With that, the man turned off the light and disappeared.

I looked down at my tiny 'gift horse' and sighed. "Well, I guess *you'll* be amusing my cats tonight."

As if to understand, he looked up at me and nodded.

I shook my head and dismissed his reaction. "I'm going to pretend I didn't see that."

As I walked through the mall with my unexpected parcel, I began to smile. "I've always wanted a fish. Maybe I'll name you Herman. Or Lou. Or how about Dennis?" I continued this discussion with myself until I arrived home. And that's when I realized—I didn't have a fish bowl.

Little Dennis sat in the bag for two hours on my bedside table while I searched the apartment for some type of container. Then I remembered my grandfather's old brandy snifter, the one I inherited when he passed away. It was big enough, perfect for my new little friend. I could use that until I bought a proper bowl. Grandpa wouldn't mind. Besides, it wasn't any crazier than him using it as a receptacle to store his teeth. Grandpa's dentures used to go for a swim every night in the brandy after he'd had dinner. The alcohol would loosen his adhesive, and after a couple sips he'd be drinking with his pearly whites staring back at him.

That memory was a funny one, I giggled at the thought of it.

I went to the hall closet and dug the bowl out of storage. "This'll work." I then took the snifter to the bathroom and cleaned it up.

Walking back to the bedroom, I realized that I hadn't seen my cats since they greeted me at the front door. Earl and Bernie, my two grey tabby cats, were my best buds. I referred to them as bumpkin snipers. The name was first coined when they saw their first spider.

I remember the day well. It started with me screaming because they were hunched in the corner of the room pawing at something. That was never a good sign; it meant that they had cornered something. I was terrified of spiders so I assumed my boys would take care of the situation. But instead, they wanted to play with it. That was fine, except the spider was supervising.

They each took turns looking at one another as if to say, "No—you get it. No—*you* get it. I don't want to touch it. It looks edible but I'm scared." The spider sat with his arms folded as he watched the two felines wimp their way out of the hunt. They were good at finding stuff but not removing it. Inevitably, I would have to find a clear glass, make sure it was absolutely stain-free so that I could see inside it, trap the animal and transfer it safely outside the walls of the apartment.

I looked out into the hallway but didn't see the cats anywhere. Where were they?

"Hey you guys, come in here and welcome our new guest," I shouted.

A moment later, two little grey heads appeared at the door.

"Come here you two. I want you to meet Dennis."

It appeared that a hidden threshold was obstructing their entry. They just sat on their haunches and stared at the silver fish swimming in the bag. They each had a strange look in their eyes. Oddly enough, it was the same look the shopkeeper gave me when I said how cute the fish was.

"What's with everyone today?"

I waited a few more minutes and then decided to open the bag and introduce Dennis to his new living quarters. Like an Olympic athlete, he leapt out of the bag and into the snifter as if he knew it was home.

For the next few hours, we watched as Dennis swam around. He seemed so happy just drifting back and forth. It appeared that he was settling in nicely. The cats had now crossed the threshold to the room but were still keeping their distance. I thought about their bizarre behaviour. It wasn't like them to avoid something new. They were both pretty curious. But something about Dennis seemed to bother them.

They each took turns creeping further into the room, but with each step they took, they puffed out their fur and retreated. It was quite funny to watch, actually. And weird, very weird.

I looked over at Dennis and thought about how empty his aquatic abode was. "You need company, I think."

Gazing around the room, I found an old, miniature toy robot from when I was young. I figured I'd give it to Dennis—anything to help make his night a little less lonely. Gently, I placed the robot in the water and watched as it sank to the bottom of the bowl. As soon as it settled, Dennis swam towards it. He circled the silver plastic toy as if he was grading it. Once he was satisfied with his new companion, he positioned himself next to it. I took that as his approval. I then sprinkled some food that the shopkeeper had given me, into the dish. Dennis didn't eat. He remained next to the toy.

Looking over at my clock, I saw that it was getting late. Time to turn out the lights. The day had ended differently than it had started, although my horoscope had said that this day would bring new acquaintances.

Tomorrow's horoscope would prove to be much scarier: Be wary of new acquaintances!

* * *

The next day started with me opening my eyes . . . and then shrieking.

Staring at me was my new fish. The bowl had apparently inched its way to the edge of the bedside table, very close to my head. I wasn't sure how something like that could've happened but I began to rationalize that maybe the cats had become more interested in Dennis after the lights were turned off. But that wasn't the scariest part. Looking at him was what startled me. His face, as narrow as it was, was full of something I hadn't imagined. He had teeth. He looked like a wet baby vampire. One look at his mouth and I was in shock. Fish weren't supposed to have fangs!

I tried to muster up a positive reaction but it was like a small newly potty trained child showing how proud he was of his own poop. "Ohhh . . . mmmy . . . . God . . . you have teeth." Was this why the shopkeeper wanted to get rid of him—because he was different? Slowly, I climbed out of the bed as my eyes remained glued to the glass. Dennis watched me closely as I crept in front of the bowl. I was absolutely stunned. I wanted to take a picture of him, but then thought about how un-motherly that would be.

The only thing I could think of to say was, "I bet you're hungry little guy." I grabbed the square container, opened it up and sprinkled some food into his bowl. "Here you go."

Dennis just stared at me. He wasn't interested in the food at all. In fact, the food from last night was still there.

I was undeniably disturbed by this point. His gaze was concrete. He was watching my every move. And that's when I realized—my toy robot wasn't in the snifter. I looked on the table and around the floor. It was nowhere to be found. "Earl, Bernie—what did you guys do with Dennis's toy?" But as I spoke the words, I saw something strange hanging from my fish's mouth.

It was a tiny, silver robot hand. "Ahh," I gasped. What the hell was happening?

"Dennis—did you eat the robot?"

He just glared at me. At that moment I was seriously wondering about what kind of mad toy-eating, fang-bearing psycho fish I had been bamboozled into taking home. Somehow, I had adopted fresh-water Chucky. Or baby Jaws rather . . . you know . . . if Jaws didn't eat organic life forms.

After the initial scare, I decided to take a different approach. I didn't want to return Dennis to the pet store because he was too intriguing. Besides, I considered myself an understanding and non-judgemental kind of person. I didn't want to prove myself incapable. I was determined to give Dennis a wonderful home and a happy life.

Then, I would call Ripley's.

First things first. I needed to wean the little guy off of plastic. Here was my approach. I would give him only his food from the container. That was it. No ifs, ands or buts. He was going to eat like a proper fish.

Well, that proposal backfired. After two days of not eating, I got worried. He wouldn't touch any of the food I gave him. He would just sit there and stare at me with grave disappointment. Then one day, I was playing with Earl and Bernie on my bed. We were batting around a small tinfoil ball when I heard a bunch of bubbles rise to the top of the snifter. I looked over and saw my little Dennis floating on the top of the water. "Oh no!" I cried. "No—you can't die, Dennis! Dennis!" I was holding the silver toy in my hand at that point when I reached over to tap the glass. Hovering over the water, I poked my fingers against his scaly skin. He didn't move. Then I accidently dropped the tinfoil ball into the water. As it descended, he sprang back to life.

The first thing he did was make a B-line straight to the shiny ball. I watched in utter disbelief as he began to inhale the foil. "Are you *serious*?" I had heard of dietary roughage but this was ridiculous.

After that, I changed his name. He was a vampire—but one that preferred toys to blood. I named him Lestat, after my favourite Anne Rice novel.

The following days were spent searching for the proper, or should I say, improper food for my little Lestat. I would go to children's stores to look at toys for my pet garbage disposal. The employees would look at me and smile, thinking that I was buying for family. Well, I was. Just not the family they were expecting.

Over the next few weeks, I learned that my little Lestat preferred Transformers to G.I. Joe. He seemed quite excited when I changed the robots into cars. And then he ate them. His favourite was Ironhide.

My cats grew to like Lestat, after realizing that their hides were unappetizing to him. Every day they would inch their way closer to his bowl. Eventually they reached the bed. They would sit for hours watching him, amused by his movements but uninterested in playing aquatic games.

At night, I would sit on the bed and read to my little swimmer. He would look up at me and smile. Of course, the books I read to him were chosen material; selected by the process of elimination. He enjoyed Grimm fairy tales more than Disney. He preferred Edgar Allan Poe over Beatrix Potter. And he absolutely adored anything science-fiction. Martians, robots, talking cars, that's what made his tiny fins flap.

My little family was a weird one but for me it was all that I needed. I looked forward to coming home from work and seeing my three boys. A cup of tea in my hands, two cats on my lap and one odd little angelfish devouring my Legos—it was a wonderful life.

And I wouldn't have wanted it any other way.

TWO

MY MONSTER

There, in the darkened aisle I stood in awe of the big, black monster. How could something this gentle behave so poorly when given the opportunity?

"Hello, Monster," I said, petting his long, furry neck. He seemed to respond to this designation as if he too had forgotten his birth name. His large ebony head leaned down towards me as if to apologize.

Juby, as the rest of the world had come to know him, was a sweet majestic, giant of a thoroughbred. He was born to race, but lacked the concept of confines. He was a rogue, a loner, an ousted equus who preferred the openness of desolate fields to a track with finite limits.

Full of spirit, he was eager to fly and ready to soar at any given moment. This behaviour however was sometimes hidden by his gentleness, a veneer that only few could see through. And apparently, I was one of the blind. His honesty was genuine though; he never once lied about that.

From the moment the monster entered my life, I felt something inside of me change. I felt driven, inspired to understand the inner thoughts of this animal if only to believe in his purpose. Thus began the challenge and thus began our story.

I looked up at him and smiled as he lifted his head. There he stood, in the dimly lit aisle of the barn, positioned between two loose nylon crossties that attached to the leather halter on his head. I laughed at the idea of crossties—they were intended for nice, sweet obedient horses that never dared to move, but not for my monster. Without notice, he could tear the other ends from the walls if he wanted to. And I knew one day he would. But today was not that day. No, today he was behaving. And for good reason—his physical outburst on our ride last week had left me with an injured tailbone and a wounded ego.

The event happened on a dark Wednesday night in the quiet of an empty arena. The monster and I had been riding around for roughly twenty minutes in perfect form, until his restlessness got the better of him. Juby took off like a wild animal, with me atop. As we ran around the empty space in pursuit of nothing but freedom, I began to lose my grip on the reins. Slowly, they slipped through my fingers as the monster turned and headed for the wall. Then without warning, his front legs lifted into the air like a trained performer from Buffalo Bill's Wild West show, and off I went to meet the end of my night.

I couldn't help but think that it was all a dream, that indeed this beautiful animal had done nothing wrong and that we were going to be the best of friends until the end of our days. But then I kept hearing it in my mind, the sound of my body violently hitting the wall—it was the last thing I remembered from that fateful ride.

Now, here he was, trying to make amends for his actions, with those big brown innocent eyes. As I looked at him, I felt a sudden calm wash over me. I was mesmerized by his beauty. His graceful presence now blurred my memory of last week's psychotic episode.

"How could I ever stay mad at you?" I asked. His sweet temperament made me question my own decision to ride again.

"Okay, Monster—let's give each other a second chance."

He snorted, as if to agree, and I leaned my head to one side, considering.

"You understand me, don't you?"

Slowly, I picked up the saddle and carefully placed it on his back. No argument. So far, so good. As I pulled the girth beneath his belly to attach the buckles, he turned his head to look at me. "That's a good monster," I said, reaching out my hand to rub his nose.

"Now it's bridle-time." But then I stopped. It was then that I felt the first wave of fear enter my system. This bridle meant business; the monster was truly in my hands once he was wearing it. Would I be strong enough to stop him if he ran loose again? Would I be brave enough to try? There was only one thing standing in my way—the courage to find out.

"I've got to do this," I told myself.

With steady hands, I removed the halter and replaced it with the bridle. As I fitted the leather straps to his head, I realized that trading one control for the other meant giving up my security blanket.

There was no looking back, the monster was now mine.

THREE

FLOWERS FLOWERS EVERYWHERE!

"Just go already—leave! Enjoy your flower show!" Henry waved at his wife.

Lilly just stared blankly at him, a vacuous gaze Henry had grown accustomed to.

"Damn petunias, daisies, carnations, orchids—they're taking over this house!" he fumed.

"They are not!" Lilly said, defensively.

"They are so! They're like your children. You've named all of them."

"So what? Why can't I name them?"

"I hate to break it to you, honey, but we don't have any children! And naming your plants doesn't count!"

"But I love each and every one as if they were my children. What's so wrong with that?"

"What's wrong with that?" Tiny tears blubbered in his eyes as they threatened to fall. "You love those plants more than you love me! And here you are off to another plant show, probably to meet some nice, handsome rose gardener for some horticultural rendez-vous!"

"How can you say that to me? I would never!"

"Oh, come on, Lilly. It's like that movie, 'The Secret Garden'. You can't trick me. I know what that movie is all about!"

Lilly smiled at her husband as she watched him slowly implode on the dining room carpet. "You're a nincompoop!" she said, crossing her arms. "And you've got the wrong movie by the way. A sick, bedridden boy and a young orphaned girl who helps him to live . . . ooh . . . ahh . . . such a deceitful affair," she cackled. "But I'm sure you're right Henry, you're always right."

His face reddened as she mocked him. "Just leave!" he pointed at the front door.

"So, I take it you're not coming then?" Lilly said, marching down the hallway. Stopping, she posed in front of the mirror.

Henry followed her closely and watched as she gingerly pressed her hair with her long fuchsia talons.

"What's happened to you, Lilly? You've gone crazy. Look at yourself. You look like a flower child—literally!" His fingers jostled in position as he pointed to the gargantuan floral arrangement stemming from her head as well as her lemon chiffon dress, which was encrusted with a layer of rose and tulip brooches. Henry could barely look at the plethora of plastic plant-life that adorned her body. "You're going to a flower show *not* Woodstock!"

Henry had realized for some time now that his wife was addicted to flowers. She collected them, bred them, raised them, but never sold them. They were slowly taking over their house *and* their lives.

Henry had seen this before, in one of those freaky movies where the blob moves into the house next door and captures the hearts of all those he meets. Everyone fawns over him while he secretly devours the neighbours one by one. But geez, say one bad thing about the blob and everyone gets mad. Just like his wife.

A smart husband, Henry had learned to stay out of his wife's path, especially when she was attending a flower show. He would simply look the other way and pretend that their marriage was rock solid. It was when he decided to attack the blob directly, that things took a turn for the worse.

Lilly on the other hand hadn't noticed any change. It was all in her husband's head, she believed. The reflection in her mirror was the same. Perhaps she was slightly more self-aware of her image but that was it. She was still the fairest of them all, the mirror had taught her that.

Henry now stared at his wife with his mouth dangling, eyes sunken, ego deflated. He had tried to make her understand that she was scaring him. But she just didn't see it.

Lilly now paced back and forth like a robot stuck in the 'on' position. Her hair stood about two feet above her head with a few tendrils escaping the sides. Shaped more like a missile, it looked like it was about to rocket right out into space. A bright green ribbon squirmed beneath the mass of blond as if it were surfacing for air. Her entire head appeared to be creating its own gravitational pull. Henry didn't want to get too close for the fear of being sucked into another galaxy. It was awkward just looking at her.

And the pull of the buzzing bee hive clearly revealed Lilly's high European cheekbones making her appear more crazed than anything. Henry thought she could pass as the bride of Liechtenstein. And her eyes! Lilly's eye lids, lashes and brows were surrounded by a peacock blue powder, so much that Henry had to squint to find them.

He was tempted now to prick her with a needle to see if she would bleed, proving that she was in fact, still human. Although he highly doubted that. Lilly was one of *them* now.

It was only a matter of time until the government found out that this alien existed and would come to take her away. And who could blame them? Perhaps they would put her under permanent surveillance or something of that sort. Or maybe they would try some new experiments—ones that weren't performed on regular humans. God knows, Henry would take part if only he had the equipment.

It didn't matter now. He had reached the end of his tether. He just couldn't wait to get this banana tree out of the house.

But more importantly, he couldn't wait to get rid of those damn flowers!

FOUR

PALMOLIVE MADE ME SPARKLE

My life was a dirty one. Clean this, clean that, scrub this, plunge that. Dust the ceilings, mop the floors, fix the garbage disposal, polish the drawers. I considered the washer and dryer twin sisters just as much as the toilet had become a good friend. We were all part of one giant working mechanism, and I was the glue that kept every piece together.

I lived in a house that operated under my command. I was the boss, the Chief, the Captain. My husband on the other hand, was the co-pilot, the assistant, the representative. Where I was Sheriff—he was Deputy. And it seemed to work. It had to, since the house had become my refuge, my sanctuary, and the only place I was allowed to work.

Here's how the story started. My husband, Ralph and I both graduated with degrees from school. His was psychology, mine was chemistry. He was hired right after graduation and given a promising position in a well-established doctor's practice.

I was not. For work, I served tables, canvassed neighbourhoods for paint jobs, slung horse manure and learned to operate the fruit squeezer at the juice stand inside the mall. The most exciting job I held—which doesn't say much—was when I handed out pamphlets for free toppings at Dairy Bling ice cream.

Needless to say, it sucked.

I dropped hot food and cold drinks onto people's laps, which admittedly, limited my serving experience to one day. I painted the wrong house, which in all fairness was as much my partner's fault as it was mine since I got completely distracted when he showed up in his underwear with a bottle of vodka in each hand. That left me looking for work that afternoon. As for my stable position cleaning stalls, I'll never understand why people didn't move when I yelled, 'Poop afloat'.

Mind you, I think my co-workers were more upset about my aim with the pitchfork. I had never seen so many people airlifted to a hospital at one time. I was fired an hour later and told something about a restraining order. That reminds me, my court hearing is in two weeks.

As for the juicing job, I almost lost a finger *and* a toe—don't ask—in the fruit squeezer, which actually made me wonder about the store's ingredient list. Let's just say I lost all faith in the Health and Safety board for the one hour that I worked there. After questioning the manager's capabilities, he had his mother come in and fire me. As a seventeen-year-old, he needed back-up and a stern spine.

But my last job at Dairy Bling took the cake—literally. After twenty minutes in the blazing sun, handing out coupons for cone toppings, I was asked to deliver an ice-cream cake to a child's birthday party. As I crossed the street to get to my car, I heard an angry engine rev behind me. Apparently the person at the wheel wasn't impressed with the pamphlet I had left on his windshield.

The car screamed out of place as it passed by me. A solitary finger extended out the window as the guy yelled out some foreign obscenity. I made it to safety, just in time to watch the idiot fly by. The cake however, wasn't so lucky.

Although it started out as a sugary-sweet symbol of happiness, it soon turned into a weapon of vehicular destruction. I lost all composure and swung the cake at the back window, brandishing the car with yellow and pink butter cream frosting. I was given my walking papers two minutes later, and a court order for causing an accident.

I was depressed, unmotivated and completely unaware of the penalty for attacking a moving vehicle. I definitely learned my lesson and a little bit about the legal system, too.

After that, I remained at home. Any thoughts of chemistry would have to wait. The house needed me and I needed the house. There, I felt safe, uninjured and entirely in charge of my surroundings and temper. Police didn't look for me, customers didn't raise complaints and desserts weren't used for combat.

Ralph became the bread-winner, while I spent the hours kneading the dough. For the time being, the house was my kingdom, my palace—my place of control. I became the cook, the plumber, the maid; I fixed everything under the roof. I pretty much had to since the ankle monitor I wore wouldn't allow me to leave the premises.

So, there I was, queen of the castle, under house arrest for attacking a man with a cake. It wasn't my most shining moment, but I was dealing with it.

As I stood now, looking out the kitchen window, washing the slime from the dishes, a smile spread across my face. I don't know whether it was the smell of green apple dish detergent that was improving my state or if I was just giddy from the oven cleanser. But for whatever reason, I felt a whole lot better. A happiness I had never felt wriggled its way into my body and made me think only wonderful thoughts.

In time, I would learn—it was the oven cleanser.

FIVE

THE CIRCUS NEEDS ME

First I learned to juggle. Then I walked the tightrope. But the moment I had to stick my head inside the jaws of a lion, I knew something at home was amiss. My life had veered off the path of normalcy and taken a hard right past the bearded lady.

Life had seemed so easy even a year ago. My twin sons and their inept big brother, aka my husband, had not yet thrown me into the fires of Mount Doom with our smaller hobbit—the cat. My husband was still employed, my sweet thirteen-year-old twinlets had not yet become teenage delinquents, and my sister hadn't left her husband to have an affair with the door-to-door marriage counsellor. This was even before my massage therapist, Hans, had flown the coop. A few weeks ago I showed up to my appointment only to be greeted by a six-foot-four Swedish man dressed as a Romulan. He wasn't much of a masseur. I wondered though, if he'd ever considered a job as a strongman.

It seemed as though every aspect of my world was deteriorating. The only thing I really clung to was our cat, Alfalfa. My husband and I had found him in the field next to our house and had adopted him into the family when he was just a kitten. We were shocked to discover that whenever anything moved, and I do mean anything, he sprouted a body wig like Diana Ross's hair in a windstorm. I had never known the true meaning of scaredy-cat until I met our little rascal. He was a source of constant amusement in our house and we loved him despite his fear of everything.

I sat now, staring at my watch, waiting for the hands to move. They seemed to take forever as they wound their way around my wrist. Then I heard a familiar voice from across the room.

"Mrs. Gregory, would you like to say something?"

I looked up and saw the daunting smile of the therapist in front of me. "No, not really."

She looked perplexed as if she hadn't expected my reply. "Are you sure? Your husband seems quite concerned with your threats of leaving. I think you should say something, whatever's on your mind."

"Well, I was just wondering how much money carneys make and if they have to pay for their own corndogs."

The room was silent. My eyes sifted through the air until they stumbled upon the man sitting beside me. His expression was hilarious. His mouth was gaped open and his eyes were in a state of disbelief.

"Honey," he said, "I don't think that's funny."

I searched my audience of two for some form of support but found none. Apparently I had stunned them. Even the portrait of Sigmund Freud hanging on the wall was in shock. I could see him shaking his head at me as he mentally scribbled my verbal concoction.

"Well, think about it," I continued. "They work hard, too, and deserve to be paid well. Especially the Tilt-a-Whirl guys. I mean come on, how many times have they had to clean up after people—especially when they've upchucked all over the rides. Around and around and around and aroooooouuuunndddd. That just doesn't sound like a word anymore, does it?" I laughed.

"Christine! This is ridiculous," my husband said. "I'm trying to talk to you about our marriage and all you're doing is making a joke of it," he trumpeted.

"I'm not making a joke of it. I'm simply stating the obvious. Carneys have a hard life and that's that."

Our therapist interjected. "Christine, I find it interesting that you keep referencing a job from an amusement park."

"It is interesting, isn't it? And what about the rubbermen—you know . . . the guys who sell balloons at the circus? I wonder what they get paid."

Our therapist stammered for a reply. I could tell she was trying to find a kind way to reconnect our derailed discourse. "I think the point your husband is trying to make is that you're avoiding the real issues in your own life. Your home life, your family life. Why don't we talk about that?"

"What's there to talk about? My life is crumbling. My husband acts like a clown. He's the one responsible for this change. Our boys need a father not a friend and that's why they get away with everything. My sister lives with us and she's not allowed to answer the door anymore because of her strange fetish with delivery men. The only member of our family that I do trust is our cat, and he's so jittery that he spends more time in the litter box than he does sleeping. So you tell me, why should I be the sane one?"

A moment passed but no words were spoken. Another moment passed. Then another.

I was not impressed. "Seriously, John," I glared at my husband, "why aren't you saying something?"

"I think your sister should move out," was all he said.

"What? *Why*?" I spewed.

"Because I don't think she's helping our situation."

"See, now I think we're getting somewhere," the therapist nodded. "John, why do you think your wife's sister isn't helping?"

This time his answer was quick. "Because *her* sister was the one who invited this whole circus into our house. She answered the door one day and started an affair with a magician. The infection then spread to Barnum and Bailey over here," he pointed to me.

I took offense to his comment. "Look, I'm not crazy. I just feel like you don't need me anymore and that some sort of change was necessary."

"No—what you need is a straight jacket," he smiled.

"Okay, Mr. Gregory—there's no need for that," the therapist said. "Try to stay positive." I could see that her occupation was evolving as the conversation continued. Soon she would be required to referee our boxing match.

"Christine, you didn't go to clown college, you went to law school for Pete's sake. You're a civil litigation lawyer. You know all about disputes between private parties . . . so why are you doing this to us?"

I smiled at him. "I still do private parties, John, just in a different capacity now."

"It's not the same thing and you know it," he said.

In the back of my mind I just couldn't understand what his problem was. To me it was simple: *he* was the problem. He just didn't get what I was going through. Everything, it seemed, was being dumped onto me, and for what? So that he could go and reclaim his youth? Was he that afraid to be the disciplinarian in the family? He had given up that role to hang out with our kids. What they needed was to be reprimanded now and then but no, he'd passed that job to me so that he could take the easy way out. And *I* was the crazy one? I don't think so.

My husband shook his head. "What about Toby and Sam? You know—*our children*? How do you think this is affecting them?"

My answer was curt. "I've been the responsible one since they were born. Not you. At least not since you lost your job. All you do is sit and play video games with them. They don't even leave the house anymore. Well, John, I've had enough. There's another family out there that needs me," I said, primping my red curls with my fingers.

John looked on and shook his head again. "You've lost it, Christine. This is insane. You need to come home and be with your family, your *real* family."

"John's right, Christine. Your family is in turmoil now and you leaving would be devastating to them. That's why he brought you here today. You may not think that you're needed right now but that's just not true. You are the monarch of your family. Your boys look up to you."

"That's a load," I laughed. "What has my husband been telling you? Did he tell you that he misplaced my work shoes? And all my make-up?"

"I didn't misplace them. The kids and I *hid* them," he said, in a controlled voice. "And what's the difference—you found them anyway."

I lifted both legs up from the ground to gaze at my polished shoes. "That's not the point."

The therapist gasped when she looked at my feet. "Christine, why don't we go back to a more positive place. How about your children? They're teenagers now and they need their mother." She looked over at John. "But they also need their father. They already have friends at school, so if you're going to help Christine get over this hump, then you're going to have to act more responsible."

"Look at us. I *am* the more responsible one. Look at my wife—just look at her! She's lost it! Put a knife in her hand and she looks like something out of Steven King's, '*IT*'!"

"Okay—if you could just refrain from name calling, that would be great," the therapist said.

"John, you just don't understand me anymore. And why should you—you're just a man!" With that I stood. The smile on my face was enough to keep me going. Gently, I smoothed the creases in my clothing.

He looked at me, his eyes now glazed over in fright. "You're not leaving! You can't leave, this is crazy!"

"No honey, it's not. Oh great, and now I'm late for work—would you look at the time! They're going to kill me if I don't get to the dunk tank by eleven."

"Mrs. Gregory, please don't leave," the therapist begged.

"C'mon," I said. "Get real! I have to go to work. Now, where is my rubber chicken?"

Coyly, my husband handed me the funny fowl. He produced it from his jacket which made me see that he was getting better at hiding things from me. He stumbled pathetically for his words. "What . . . have . . . they . . . done . . . to . . . you?"

I turned to face the floor-length mirror in the corner of the therapist's office. All I saw was perfection. My yellow and blue striped uniform beamed brightly from the light shining through the window. The tight red curls from my wig accented the smooth leather of my crimson shoes. And the chicken I now held dear accompanied the belt of coloured handkerchiefs around my waist. The giant painted smile that I wore reassured me that I was doing the right thing.

As I pulled my nose out of my pocket, I had an epiphany. I could be the best clown ever. People from far and wide would come to see me and why? Because I represent the circus.

I twirled my body to flaunt my outfit in front of the mirror. "Don't I look stunning?"

There was no response.

I turned to face the double audience. "Well—don't I?"

Both patrons jumped in their seats.

"You know, I think the saddest thing in the world is a sad clown. You wouldn't want to make me sad, would you? Because I could show you the old iron-jaw trick," I stared at the man in the front row.

He tossed his head from side to side. "No—I wouldn't want you to do that."

"That's more like it!" My eyes brimmed with a cheerful gloss. "Now, let's get this show on the road. Ballyhoo!"

No other zanies, pongers, kinkers or towners could save me.

I had finally found my way to the Big Top.

SIX

MY SIDE OF THE WALL

It was typical. I could hear my family talking about me while I listened in. It was a good thing that the walls in our house were paper thin because they did this to me all the time—talked about my reckless lifestyle, my unfortunate fashion sense, and the way I sped through life as if I were in a race to find my future before anyone else did. Maybe they were right.

The only problem was that they were still treating me as if I were nine years old, forcing me into another room while they deliberated my fate. Back then I wasn't privy to my own shortcomings; apparently they were selected by my parents and my two older siblings, Ryan and Josie.

My family told me that I was a wild child who needed every bit of preventative fencing possible. Perhaps they were worried I was going to hurt myself. True, I liked to venture down abandoned roads on my bicycle for hours alone. But that didn't mean I wasn't coming back, it just meant that I was coming back on a different day and usually with various coloured spots from my acts of fearlessness. And then there was the time I skipped two days of high school to go see my favourite rock band with my friends in a neighbouring city. But that act of independence didn't mean that I disrespected my teachers, it just meant that there was a need for improvement and compromise in my school's scheduling. It was as simple as that.

But things had changed. Time had changed. I wasn't nine years old or even a high school student anymore. I had slowed down on the path to my future and had grown up into a woman with cares and responsibilities.

It all happened the year I turned nineteen. The year my world changed forever.

I had taken a year off from life to figure out how I was going to live. It wasn't a particularly foreign concept, but with so many interests in this world, it was hard for me to narrow down the suspects. I knew that I wanted a university education, to attain a degree in something, but what exactly? I loved astronomy, history and biology—those were the top contenders.

The next step was to match them against each other in my mind and have them battle it out in the boxing ring. Then I would have my answer. Here's how it ended: the Trojans battled the birds and the bees but then the cosmos blew them both out of the sky. Astronomy it was.

Of course, I could tell only my family about my weird little analogies. No one else would understand. My father used to say that I was the perfect blend of crazy and nuts. But I loved him anyway.

I had applied to three different universities, one of them being a local school just a short commute away. I was excited and nervous at the same time. Chamomile tea became a daily tonic to calm my anticipation.

Eagerly, I awaited news of my acceptance, harassing the mailman each morning with ruthless smiles until he too gave into my excitement.

Then the day arrived.

I awakened to the sound of my mom knocking on my bedroom door.

"Mags, are you awake?"

I could hear myself mouthing the words with a yawn. "Yep. I'm up mom."

"Mags, I need to talk to you."

"Come on in, Mom. What's on your mind?"

"Well," she said opening the door, "we need to talk about your doctor's appointment."

"Uh huh," I slurred, with my eyes still closed.

"Maggie, this is serious. Wake up sweetie."

Although I was considered both the wild child and the black sheep of the family for the most part, I still loved my mom's terms of endearment for me. I was still the baby of the family and that stood for something, regardless of my unruly past.

There she was however, driven more than ever to save me from myself. A beautiful woman with unwavering support for her baby girl. I loved her for that.

"Maggie, you've taken the initiative to apply to universities and your father and I are very proud of you. You know that, right?"

"Of course, Mom."

"And we're so happy that you've found a stable path to set your goals on."

I watched as a tear dripped down her cheek. "Mom, why are you crying? I thought you were happy for me. I'm finally doing something positive with my life."

She wiped the tear away with the cuff of her blouse. "Of course I'm happy for you, Mags. The entire family is."

"Then, what's the problem? Why are you so upset?"

For a moment, she was silent.

"Mom, I've known about the test results for days. You don't have to tell me." The tears just poured down her face faster. Mom, we were expecting this, remember?"

"I know, Mags . . ."

"So, let me deal with this. I know you all want to protect me but you have to understand that I'm an adult now. Not telling me first about the results made me feel like a kid again. And it still does."

"Is that how you knew?"

"Yes, Mom, that's how I knew. You all had a family meeting while I listened on the other side of the wall. You never realized that I could hear everything—the walls are really thin."

"Mags, it's just . . . that . . . we didn't know how to tell you. Your father answered the phone, he was the one who spoke to the doctor. We didn't know that you were listening."

I smiled at my mother. "This is *my* future we're talking about, correct?"

She nodded in agreement.

Did she finally understand? Had it really taken this long for her to realize that her little girl was now a woman in search of control?

"Mom, that's why I wanted a new future, something I could believe in. I've always been the free spirit of the family. I climbed trees, broke lots of bones, took plenty of risks. I can handle this. Out of everyone in our family, I was meant to have this because I'm the one who takes chances. My life has already been full of accidents and surprises. This is just another hurdle."

"Maggie, we just want to take care of you, make sure that you're safe. But I guess that's not up to us anymore, is it?"

I shook my head and looked into her eyes. "Mom, I'm not a kid anymore. I will always be your baby, but I'm not a kid anymore."

"Okay, then. Why don't you tell me more about the universities you applied to," she said, wiping away another tear. "I want to hear more about your studies."

So, there we sat on my childhood bed talking about dreams, goals, life and my future. It was a conversation I would remember forever.

Throughout the following week, I fretted and waited for the postman, anxious for a letter of acceptance, dreading the possibility that all three universities might turn me down. I found myself looking for any sort of physical distraction. I rode my bike, went shopping, cleaned my room many times over, and hiked through the nearby park as much as possible. It felt great to get my mind off of my impending future. I spent hours just sitting on the swings in the neighbourhood park my parents used to take me to as a kid. Back and forth I swayed while my feet floated through the air. This helped my thoughts escape any looming letters or results.

Then, Thursday came along.

I was lying on the sofa in the family room, watching an episode of *The Dukes of Hazard* on the television, when the doorbell rang. I stood up and slowly made my way into the hallway, toward the front door. And that's when it hit me: this was it!

I could see the mailman through the window beside the door. He was grinning.

At that moment I heard Ryan running for the door. "I got it," he said gliding past me. "Sorry Mags, I'm waiting for something. It's supposed to arrive today." He must have seen my disfigured expression, for he notably stated, "What's with the gnarly face? I won't hog the mail, kiddo. Relax."

He opened the door and exchanged pleasantries with the mailman as I looked on from the hallway. It was then that I felt a wave of nerves overcome me and I couldn't bring myself to step any further.

Unfortunately, that was the last thing I remembered. After that moment, things changed for me. The future that I had so desperately sought, revolted and turned on me. This life of mine was now headed in a new direction—one that I had not desired nor intended.

My life darkened from that moment on.

I could see the stars above me, guiding my body onto a new path. I heard the distant sounds of sirens as I passed by the brilliant lights. Each step I took felt like an eternity, as if my legs were being pulled from the earth like a tree. Adventurous as I was, there was now something inside of me holding me back. I understood fear for the first time. There was a heavy weight in my heart and I felt a shadow of pain slowly pass over my body. Then I felt nothing. And for the longest time I remained still.

I had questions, many in fact, but I was now alone with only my thoughts.

The anticipation of my future had pushed me into a trance, intoxicating me with feelings I had not bargained for. Perhaps the weight of my scholastic destiny was too much for me to bear. My shoulders were well on their way to expanding but maybe they just weren't strong enough yet.

A reaction like this did seem a little dramatic especially to a harmless letter designed of paper and ink. But it was a natural reaction, unscripted and honest.

As I listened carefully to my inner thoughts, I heard a subtle voice enter my ears. It was familiar; I identified it immediately. It was my brother Ryan. The pitch in his voice revealed his concern. Had he accidentally opened one of my letters instead of his? I would have to kill him if he did—I'd been waiting for those letters for months now. I tried to listen to what he was saying, but his speech was blurred. That darn brother of mine, he probably opened my letters on purpose just so that he could read them first.

Just then I heard a woman's voice, very faint.

"Can she hear us?"

Hmm . . . a female voice talking down to me, it could only be my sister Josie. I bet she was in on it, too, trying to steal my thunder by opening my letters before me. Strange siblings of mine. Why couldn't the members of my family just leave my personal life alone? That would be a question for another time perhaps. Right now I just had to focus.

"She was accepted," another voice spoke. And I knew right away that it was my mother. But for some reason her voice seemed different. In fact all of their voices seemed different, somehow.

"One of those happy days," a man said.

It was my dad. He was here, too.

"I was accepted?" I shouted in excitement. "Oh wow! Ryan—it's okay. I'm not mad at you for opening my letters. I can't believe it, I'm going to school. I'm going to have a future after all!"

"She deserves it," Josie said. "Mags worked hard to get into school. She finally got her act together. What unbelievable timing."

"Josie, Josie—aren't you proud of me? I'm going to school!"

There was no reply. I was wondering what had happened to the excited state of my family. But now there was only silence.

"Aren't you all happy for me?"

The air was still, no sound.

"This is a positive step for me, isn't it wonderful?"

Nothing. No response.

"Isn't anyone listening to me?"

Then I realized, it was just like when I was kid and the rest of my family was on the other side of the wall. But there was no getting over this wall.

Life is a funny thing. Just when you think you've got a handle on it, you lose your grip. And for me, that's pretty much what happened.

For months my family had come to the hospital to visit me in my state of rest. Over time they watched as my body slowly deteriorated from the leukemia that had taken over this life. At first, I could hear their voices, but then they slowly faded. As it turned out, my future was governed by something I could not fight nor wrestle nor defeat.

This wall could not be breached, but finally I was at peace on my side of it.

SEVEN

CURSE OF THE LUNCH LADY

There she stood in all her glory. My arch nemesis—the lunch lady. Oooohh she was a fearsome ogre. And cruel too. A culinary robot designed for one purpose only: to destroy each and every spoonful of my high school experience. Mrs. Witairns was her name and killing my appetite was her game. Mrs. Pithairs was the nickname I had coined and for good reason too. When she lifted her arms, out sprang an army of hidden troops. And I swear to you that if a hair popped out, you just knew it was headed for the food. The food *I* was about to eat.

Her name also reminded me of the Pitcairn islands, from a movie I had watched with my dad. And it gave me ideas. Mutiny against the lunch lady was all I had dreamt about these last few years.

She was the scariest of all educational hitmen because her position aroused no suspicions. Feeding the masses was her job. But I knew better. Once that lunch bell struck twelve, students would run to the cafeteria, drawn by the smells of freshly cooked mush, not even knowing that they were in the hands of a supervillain. She was like Lex Luther with giant boobs and a Cuisinart.

But as much as I had suffered from Mrs. Pithairs trying to poison me, I resented her most of all for her total lack of responsiveness. Way back on my first day of grade nine, I had struck her with my prettiest smile—a smile that had been making grownups go gaga since before I can remember. I'd said "Hello, good afternoon," in my cheeriest voice.

And Mrs. Pithairs' response? A look of such indifference as to rival a dead fish. Then with a gesture of her finger, she directed my attention to the "food." I think I screamed.

Ever since that day, throughout my entire high school career, I've tried to get a response out of Mrs. Pithairs. But so far, nothing. Not a single reaction.

That was all about to change because today, I was bolstered with determination.

I stood now, at the back of the line, leaning against the wall. I was watching all the poor defenceless cattle in front of me as they each made their way to the food trough. They slithered closer to the counter. One by one, fear entered their eyes as they realized what their menu options were. And it couldn't have been more scary.

First in the line-up was a tray full of brown plop. It resembled horse manure and sadly, was the nicest of all the coloured foods available. Next was a platter filled with green stringy booger blings. I think it was a vegetable but I wouldn't stake my life on it. The following two trays were filled to the brim with yellow pasty vomit-textured barf bilge. It looked like creamed corn—without the corn. Oh she was a crafty one. There were a few unmentionable items in between but the last of the trays contained a bright red soupy substance which I could only imagine as blood from the last student who gave her grief.

Those were the choices. And that is where she had us. Mrs. Pithairs controlled our stomachs and in doing so—controlled our lives.

I watched carefully as each frightened adolescent closed their eyes and pointed to the slosh they would soon down. Sad faces, all of them. But not me. Not today. I was wearing a smile. I had big plans for this supervillain. This was going to be my day of retribution. Okay, so maybe *this* mutiny would be a sole effort but that was alright. I could make it work.

I remembered going home yesterday and feeling the wrath of my stomach as it demanded a reason for why I abused it so. I could feel it rejecting the food I had eaten at lunch. My mind and intestines were battling each other as I strained to keep down the blue sludge I had forced into my system hours earlier. *Why on Earth were the tacos blue?* I asked myself over and over again. I knew it was a bad idea to eat them, but at that time I had no other option. Besides, I convinced myself that it was all fodder for retaliation.

I later told my parents that I would no longer eat food from the cafeteria. All I wanted from that point on in my life was a home-made lunch in a brown bag, made with my mother's love. Food with shape was most coveted: edges, layers, starting points and end points. These were characteristics I desperately desired in my meals.

But of course my timing was off. In order for my plan to work, I would have to eat from the cafeteria one more time. This was going to work, I just knew it. This was my mission impossible. All I had to do now was get into character. Ahead of me, someone in the line muttered, "I think I'm going to be sick." And I knew right then and there that it was time.

Slowly, I pulled a small sandwich bag from my pants pocket. Inside the bag was a blood-ridden ratty old bandage that I had doctored the night before. It was beautiful. I'm not one for bragging, but just looking at it made me realize I was headed for a career as a make-up artist for horror movies. Carefully I looked around to make sure that I was not being watched. With my other hand, I reached into the opposite pocket and pulled out another baggie. Inside this one was a chopped plastic finger that I had bought at the bargain store. This was my coup de grace. I knew this one would finish her off. *Muah ah ah,* I laughed to myself. But then I looked around to make sure no one had heard me. My criminal mind was to be kept a secret.

Without drawing any attention, I gently took the items out of the bags and threw the bags into the nearest garbage can. It was important that I discarded them—I'm pretty sure that I saw that somewhere on CSI. I kept the bloody bandage and plastic finger cupped in my hands as I began to walk towards the line of students. One by one they ambled towards the counter as I now stood behind them, waiting. Evil thoughts raged through my mind, like what I was going to do when . . . . *Wait a minute,* I stopped. *I'm not the villain here.* I had to remind myself of that.

I could feel the devilish lure of Mrs. Pithairs as I got closer. Up ahead I could see her black hair squished beneath a tight little hairnet as it tried to contain the horns hidden within. Every part of her was wicked, from her pitchfork to her cloven hooves. The grim expression she wore was an indication that Satan himself was somewhere nearby. It was enough to frighten anyone or anything. There were times I thought, when even the food looked scared.

The line began to move. Now there were only nine victims in front of me. Then it would be my turn to face the beast. This was going to be a good day. I could feel the smile return to my face.

"But I don't think that looks like vegetarian stew," a meek voice rattled from the front of the line. When I looked up, I saw the disturbed expression of a female student as she tried to discern what exactly she had been served.

The line moved.

"Why is the apple pie green?" a male student questioned. There was no answer. Just a reluctant acceptance of a dessert he was unsure of eating.

The line moved.

"I have dietary restrictions," a blond-haired senior student said. "I can't have dairy because I'm lactose intolerant. I can't have eggs because I don't believe in eating anything yellow. I'm allergic to shellfish and peanuts. And I can only have a certain amount of calories per meal."

Uh oh, I thought. This was a zit just waiting to be popped. The girl gave a surprised yelp when she was handed a knife, a fork and a piece of cardboard, then told to move on.

The next few students took their food without question. Once receiving their meals, they turned and scurried away for fear that they would be offered seconds.

Four students. Three students. Two students to go. Then me.

As the last student before me scrambled towards the counter, I felt a shiver tingle up my back. I could see the robot, the beast, the devil, standing behind the plastic counter. Sure the divider separated us from her but what about the food—what about their protective rights? I could see her glaring down the guy in front of me. He wore a cheery smile and said, "Good afternoon," as he approached her.

She, of course said nothing. Her black eyes were doing all the talking and 'I hate you' was all they said. I giggled to myself. I figured he must be a new student. Boy was he going to get it.

His grin soon disappeared as a look of concern covered his face. I could see it—he was trying to figure out a way to connect with her so that she wouldn't spit in his food when he wasn't looking. It was sad really.

It was like watching a lion ambush its prey.

This kid didn't know what he was up against. He was uncertain of everything that was on display before him and so he started to ask. "Could you . . . tell . . . me . . . um . . . what that yellow stuff is? Is it . . . potatoes or corn?" His voice started to jiggle. "And . . . um . . . that red . . . ahh . . . umm . . . stuff over there . . . is that . . . vegetable soup?"

It was like watching a python suffocating a field mouse.

A few minutes passed but the poor guy finally succumbed to the torturous stare of Mrs. Pithairs. Sweat dripped from his forehead as his hands began to shake. "Um . . . well . . . I guess I'll take a bit of each—it all looks so good."

And there it was—his last attempt at keeping his knees from knocking together. He had put up a good fight too but it was time to accept defeat.

I had seen it so many times before. I walked up behind him and patted him on the shoulder. He looked back at me and frowned. "I don't even know what this stuff is but I'm afraid to say anything."

I gave a knowing look of empathy. "It's okay, buddy. It's okay."

Staring at the tray of unknown food in his hands, he dragged his defeated appetite to one of the tables and hung his head.

Poor guy. He showed so much promise. But when I looked back, I saw the eyes of the monster in front of me and I jumped back into action. My time had come. Oh, how I waited for this day. And now here I was, ready for battle.

I looked into her beady little eyes and stared. We met each other's glare, neither of us moved.

"I see you have the usual suspects for us today," I said, nonchalantly.

There was no answer. Only her silent angst for those of us who dared speak aloud about her food.

I quickly gazed down by her side and saw her equally unforgiving partner in crime—the ladle. Oh, I hated the ladle. But I guess if it weren't for him, Mrs. Pithairs would be using her hands to dish out our punishment. That was much more her style anyway.

"And I can see that the mould hasn't yet occupied the entire counter-top. That's a nice touch." My feet were firmly planted and my confidence was unwavering.

I was ready with another one. "No one's died from the rat poison in the pudding yet. How lucky for you."

Still nothing. Not a tweak, not a peep, not even a twinge. For a moment I wondered if she was still alive. But she was a robot—I had to remember that. Anyone else would have at least giggled or said something. Anything. Any sort of retort would have been appreciated. But I had to stick to the plan. I couldn't get side-tracked.

"I'll have the brown, the yellow and a bit of the green."

Up came the ladle like a gun from its holster. In record-breaking time, she transported the edible crud from serving tray to plate and then handed it to me. I took the tray and set it on the horizontal rails in front of me. I didn't want to look away but I had to for a moment. I pushed the tray along as I opened my one hand and dropped the finger and bandage into the food. I spun the items with my fork as I mixed everything together. I then looked back at her.

"So, I heard that one of the students went missing last week. It was right after he ate lunch. Here. In the cafeteria. I guess he must have eaten your sloppy Joes. Is that what's left of him?" I pointed to the red syrupy soup. "Jason—is that you?" I tapped the plastic divider.

Nothing. Nada. No response. Not even a grin. Not even a chuckle.

I looked down at my food, and as I stood to take a mouthful of coloured puke, I screamed. "Ahh—a finger! Oh my God it's a finger! And . . . oh no . . . it's a bloody bandage! I can't believe this! Ahh!"

Everyone in the lunch room looked up in alarm. One girl screamed a deafening cry, "A finger? Oh my God!" Another student gagged, spewing his food back onto the plate. Around me was a look of horror. Then one by one, each terrified cafeteria-goer rummaged frantically through their food in search of hidden contamination. Unsatisfied with their witch hunt, the room then turned into a frenzied fear of teenage doomsday as the students ran for the doors in a chaotic mess. Screams echoed all around as their arms waved madly about in search of safety.

Awesome . . . wicked . . . perfect, I thought.

Gazing back at Mrs. Pithairs, I could tell she was not impressed. She just glared at me, and then dismissively rolled her eyes.

"Not even a smirk?" I asked.

Nothing. Zilch. Damn.

"I got nothing for that?" I couldn't believe it. I tried so hard to make this scheme work and got nothing for it. Not a single thing. She was impossible! At that moment she was elevated to the status of 'Alien'.

I was disturbed and flustered, but came to the conclusion that Mrs. Pithairs would never give me the response I needed.

Reluctantly, I accepted defeat.

"Fine—I'll just grab my drink and be on my way. Thank you for the four years of insufferable torment that came with eating your food, and for being kind enough to dole out your punishment in rations."

It was the last thing that I said to her. But before I walked away, I heard a voice behind me say, "That's the first time anyone's ever thanked me."

Turning back, I saw Mrs. Pithairs' timid smile peeking through her face. I had never seen her smile before—I didn't even know she owned one. I had tried so hard to get a response from her. All those years. All those horrific years.

When all it took was a thank you!

EIGHT

STUFFED

Mandy let out an unexpected gasp when the front door opened. Looking around, she shuddered.

"Come on in," Herman invited her. He giggled to diffuse his awkwardness. "I'm not used to having guests over."

Mandy remained in place. She was having a hard time just stepping over the welcome mat which was covered with spiders, frogs and bats. Peering into the house, she sighed. "I'm starting to see that." And for Mandy, it was all starting to sink in.

At dinner, Herman seemed just a tad unusual, just a tad. But it *was* their second date, maybe he was just nervous. Perhaps the restaurant they'd gone to was too overwhelming. But the first date had gone quite well, and that reassured her.

Her quest started roughly three weeks earlier when Mandy decided to take control of her love life and join an internet dating website. She'd had enough of her mother's meddling. In the last year alone, her mother had introduced her to seven men, all of whom were victims of their own mothers' meddling.

Seven dates. Seven rejections.

The first was with a banker. They met. They ate. He ended up at the hospital when his head expanded to the size of a balloon. Needless to say, he was allergic to something. It could have been the shellfish, or the peanuts, or the strawberries, or the chocolate. There was a list of things he wasn't supposed to eat which included pretty much everything within the realm of Earth. Mandy left him at the hospital and never looked back, except to steal the pudding from his dinner tray.

Date two was with a gorgeous, fabulously dressed gay man who spent the whole time fixing her hair while bashing the latest celebrity wardrobe violators. They remained friends afterwards but that was about it.

The third date was over before it started when Mandy noticed that all the silverware was missing from the restaurant table. Her date smiled and explained how he had a fetish for building castles out of cutlery, and couldn't afford his own. She politely excused herself from the table and then escaped through the bathroom window.

Date number four was mildly uninteresting, except for the fact that the man she met left her company with an odd smile and an unexpected parting gift of food poisoning. At least the medics had arrived quickly.

For date five, Mandy met her mate at Captain Logan's Fish Hut. Apprehensive at first, she reminded herself that it couldn't be that bad. She was wrong. A young man with a receding hairline and a wooden peg-leg joined her at the table with a bucket full of fried fish. She stayed, out of mere intrigue, to watch the swashbuckling relic act his way through the night. Had it not been for the stuffed parrot doing all the talking, the date would have been a nautical washout. But after the fifth 'shiver me timbers', she decided to leave.

Date six started off well. The restaurant was nice. Dinner was nice. The conversation was nice. But the man was still married and longed for an additional relationship. After Mandy discovered his fetish for female escorts, he was rushed to the hospital to have the fork removed from his leg.

Man number seven seemed promising, until he returned from the bathroom wearing make-up, perfume and a wig. Turns out, he was a drag queen for Thelma's Hot and Spicy cabaret bar downtown. The most disturbing part is that he was preparing a Captain and Tennille tribute concert. The scary part—he was Tennille.

Yes, Mandy had finally had enough. She realized that her love life was not safe in the hands of family. If she was to find someone appropriate, she would have to do it herself.

In enters Herman.

Mandy found him on an internet dating website entitled, 'Love Forever—Who Knew!' She coerced herself into joining and immediately found three men of interest. After chatting with all three, she narrowed down her list. One lived too far away and the other had a job that was too time-consuming. But the one that was left seemed perfect.

Herman Hatfield. A landscaper by profession, with his own house, in a nice neighbourhood nearby. He was six-foot-three, with brown hair and soft blue eyes. Mandy was immediately interested in him.

On their first date, they met at a coffee shop. For hours they sat sipping, connecting, smiling, laughing. It was the best date Mandy had been on for quite some time. She was in heaven, Herman was perfect.

When they parted, he gave her a traditional peck on the cheek to instill his interest and remind her of his sincerity.

Mandy was smitten. Date one—success! Finally, a man worth meeting.

Date two. Herman picked Mandy up at her house and took her out for dinner to a fancy restaurant. Mandy acknowledged his state of anxiety and calmed his nerves with gentle glances and humorous anecdotes. He found her both charming and soothing. It was a fitting union, a relationship ideal for both.

And then Herman invited her back to his place.

Mandy stood now by the door, looking down at the mat. *Oh good God, what have I gotten myself into?* she wondered.

"Mandy, come on in. I want to introduce you to some of my family."

With great hesitation, she stepped over the threshold and entered into the dwelling.

Herman's house looked more like a jungle than anything else. Several eight foot tree-like plants were scattered across the front room. Vines were growing rampant along the walls and flowers emerged from all over.

After the initial scare, Mandy began to rationalize. *He is a landscaper, and who doesn't take their work home with them? A lot of people like plants.* Her thoughts distracted her from the fact that Herman had momentarily disappeared.

She heard his voice reappear in the room and that's when her fears jumped a notch. "Ahh!"

she screamed. "What . . . what is that?" Her arm jiggled as she pointed to the object in his hands.

"Oh this," he laughed. "This is George."

Mandy stared at the statue-like animal resting between his fingers. "Is he . . . dead?"

"Yes, he is." Herman said with a smile. "I found him in the park one day. He was already gone. But I still felt like he needed a home."

By this time, Mandy was already calculating her running distance to the door. "That's . . . a squirrel . . . a dead squirrel."

"Yeah . . . isn't he cute?"

Mandy didn't quite know what to say. "You have . . . a dead squirrel in your home . . ."

"One of many," Herman winked.

That's when Mandy started to back up. Not looking, she bumped into one of the trees behind her. The leaves shook and out fell a small, yellow bird.

"Ahh!" She jumped back in surprise.

"Oh, be careful. That's Patrick. He's two years old and quite the cantankerous little fellow." Herman ran over to pick him up. He lifted the bird and wagged his finger at his beak. "Now, Patrick, you be nice to our house guest. You know how seldom we have them." He looked up at Mandy and laughed. "Honestly—who teaches manners anymore?"

Mandy stared at him. *How could I have missed this? How could I have not seen this side of him?*

She gazed across the room and that's when they appeared. Hidden in the trees, perched on the vines, sitting on the windowsills—animals of all shapes and sizes. And all of them—dead!

Christopher, the Cuckoo in mid-flight. Matthew, the Mole, frozen in mid-crawl. Randy, the rattlesnake, dangling from the tree. Peggy, the porcupine, poking out from behind the curtain. All had names. All were stuck in mid-pose. All were freaking her out.

"This is my family, Mandy."

She opened her mouth to say something, but only air escaped.

"Biff likes to open windows when I'm not home, don't you, Biff? He's a Vesper bat and likes to go outside at night. And Nadine over there, well she's a crocodile newt and loves to party. Isn't that right, Nadine?"

"Wait just a minute," Mandy yelled. "Are you telling me that you stuffed all these animals . . . and now they're your family?"

Herman looked around the room and then nodded. "I thought that was obvious." He held a small rabbit in his hands as his fingers slid over its furry head. "Taxidermy is a passion of mine. But I can't take credit for all of them. Some of them I bought from other collectors. Why—is something wrong?"

Mandy looked at the rabbit and then at Herman. "Yes . . . yes something's wrong. You're petting a dead rabbit!"

"Hey . . . this isn't just any rabbit. This is Felix! He's a New England Cottontail, and might I add, one that deserves a little respect!"

"What?! That's crazy. The rabbit's dead, Herman . . ."

"Don't talk to him like that, Mandy! He's my family, although a couple times removed," he giggled.

Mandy's eyes were bulging, her mouth gaping.

"And so is Elvis, my Mountain Pygmy possum, and Bertha, my Brazilian tapir."

Mandy couldn't understand how a man so seemingly normal could act this way. Unfortunately, she had not yet experienced the full wrath of his obsession. But then she saw something sitting behind one of the trees. Stepping closer, her eyes widened. Another gasp exited her pale lips. A family of rats sitting at a small table took her breath away. Each one was dressed in doll's clothing and positioned around the table drinking tea.

That was the straw that broke the camel's back.

Herman had no chance to explain. Before he knew it, a whirling wiz of air flew past him as Mandy bolted towards the front door. In an instant, she was gone.

Mandy was stuffed herself, full of anger, full of resentment for not being able to find someone normal, or even natural from this universe.

One week later, she returned to the internet site and with determination in her heart, began her search again.

This time she came across a young man who appeared handsome, smart and strong. His profile picture showed him holding a butterfly in his one hand. She considered his profession, Insect Biology? Grinning from ear to ear, she thought, *Maybe this could be the one!*

NINE

FOR THOSE OF US WHO COULDN'T SERVE

"It's okay, Gracie," the blonde said from across the room. She was sitting in a chair that squeaked every time her body leaned to the left, and it was driving me crazy. I called her Squeaky-McSqueakerson. She deserved the hyphen.

Her real name was Cheryl. She was perky, sunshiny bright and high maintenance. I could tell. She was one of those people who dressed to code, meaning: her shoes matched her lipstick, which matched her purse, which matched her personality. Good grief. And her voice, oh God, her voice. It was so shrill and high-pitched that I'm sure somewhere on the planet a family of sea lions were calling her back home. I wished at that very moment I had a bucket of fish to shut her up.

"Gracie. Can you hear me?" she said with a concerned smile.

I realized then that I had slid into a different mental state. Encapsulated in my own thoughts, I had forgotten where I was. Looking around, my eyes took in the surroundings. Forming a rather large circle in a small, unsightly room, were twenty red and blue chairs that were stained with what I hoped was coffee. Nineteen pairs of judgemental eyes stared back at me. Their bodies sat motionless and quiet, distanced from each other as they waited for me to speak. Well, except for Ted, whose face was slightly obstructed by the finger that was up his nose.

The others wore the same expression Squeaky-McSqueakerson did. Their eyebrows were lifted and their mouths were still. All of them were probably wondering what was wrong with me. I guess it was time to tell them.

I locked eyes with Squeaky and she nodded to me. "Really—it's all right, Gracie. We're here to listen and help. It's okay to talk to us. That's why you're here. And that's why we're here."

She gazed around at the group and grinned. "We're going to help each other through our trials and difficulties. Our meetings do work." She then motioned me onward with her hand. "So, Gracie, let's hear your story."

I had crawled into the class late and had only caught the tail-end of someone else's story. It had something to do with food, setting tables I think. I noticed that most of the other people in the group had their hands either tucked into their laps or their arms crossed. And it seemed as though they were safely distanced from one another which seemed odd to me, being a support group and all. But I didn't care about that. I only cared about getting help.

"Well . . . to start . . . I have anxiety." I heard the harmonic tones of everyone around me as they affirmed my statement in unison. I could tell they all harbored some anxiety as well. *Hmm,* I thought. *Maybe they will understand.*

"When I started my last job, I figured I could keep my anxiety at bay. I was nervous—like everyone else on their first day, but I told myself to keep a positive state of mind. I did my best to believe it."

Squeaky reassured me with two thumbs pointed up. "That's a wonderful way to start out."

Brushing off her plastic enthusiasm, I continued my story. "But that didn't last. I had practiced with trays at home, carrying drinks and such from one table to another to see how I performed. It was unsettling how bad I was."

Many of those around me now lowered their heads in sympathy. It was as if they knew what was coming. "So, for my first day of work, I arrived early. Happy. Willing. Medicated."

I took a deep breath as I prepared to unleash the horror onto all these poor people surrounding me. "Well, it was a new medication, I had just switched pharmacies. The restraining order against me wouldn't allow me to go near the old one. Apparently the pharmacists don't like it when you raise your voice to them. Nor do they like it when you rip open the condom packages, fill them with cough syrup, jump on the counter and toss them like baseballs. But see, that's why I needed my medication. I'm prone to psychotic episodes."

A few heads in the room lifted at those last few sentences. I could feel the judgement begin.

"But once I got my medication at the new pharmacy, I behaved myself. Everything was fine."

Squeaky's enthusiasm slowly faded as the curl from her effervescent smile began to straighten.

I gave a delightful nod and then continued. "Problem was, they gave me the wrong dosage."

Two more heads lifted up.

"So, here I was on the first day of my new job, on a new medication that was basically putting me in overdrive. My nerves were heightened and my senses were alive with vitality. I felt like I could do no wrong. And I told myself, 'You can do this, Gracie. You can!' even though I had never waited on people before. But the restaurant was in desperate need of staff. Also, I had lied on my resume and told the employer that I'd worked in a restaurant setting before. In a non-existent town. For three non-existent years. But I needed a job and wanted to prove to myself that I possessed the skills necessary to do it."

Three more heads lifted.

"God, I remember it like it was yesterday. It was my first table—a young couple, mid-twenties. They were on their first date together. They told me that when I took their drink order. Unfortunately the medication made me a little flippant. That, combined with my natural tendency towards clumsiness, was a recipe for disaster."

A woman in the room gasped and then coughed. After taking a swig of water she apologized and sunk back in her chair.

"Well, I forgot about their order completely when I accidently dropped the empty tray on the woman sitting behind them. When I leaned down to get it, our heads knocked together and my barrette got entwined in her wig. If only I hadn't pulled back so hard, she would still be wearing her hair. As covertly as possible, I placed the wig back on her head and apologized while making a discreet exit from the table."

Squeaky's lips were starting to furl downward instead of up. Perhaps she hadn't heard a story like mine before. Oh well, whatever. I was just getting started.

"When I came back with their drinks, my two left feet decided it was time to meet. This unfortunate union forced the glasses into the air like a flying circus act. The drinks landed sideways and poured onto the laps of my innocent patrons. Thank God they were wearing napkins. The apologies spewed from my mouth as I tried to get a handle on my nerves. Backing away was the only redeeming quality I had to offer at that moment."

As I was leading up to the appetizer portion of my story, I could see the remaining heads in the room lift. Many of the people sitting in the circle now had strange looks on their faces. It seemed as though they were not amused by my antics. Funny though, since they were all here for the same reason I was. They couldn't serve tables either.

With another deep, penetrating breath, I moved on to the next part of my four course story.

"Well, my boss at this point says to me, 'Don't worry, everyone has it rough in the beginning.' It sounded like a lie but I had to agree with him since I was supposed to have done this sort of work before—as per my forged resume. So, I make another attempt with the drinks but as you now know I'm not very coordinated and this time I don't make it past the bar before dropping both drinks on the floor. My timing is the real issue here because Sid, who no longer is a friend of mine, walks past me and skids on the ice. He skated halfway across the floor into the kitchen door which unfortunately dislodged one of his front teeth. Lucky for me, his anger was stifled when the door burst open and Heather charged through carrying two large trays of food. Sadly for him, the slamming of the door against his face broke his nose."

A single, solitary giggle erupted from one of the men sitting in the circle. Squeaky quickly vanquished his response with a harsh finger over her mouth.

"And well, after the medics arrived, things returned to normal. By this time, the young couple had declined all drinks and had politely moved on to stationary food. The kitchen had prepared their appetizers and I was on my way to their table to serve them when . . ."

"When *what?*" a young woman said five chairs over. It appeared as though she couldn't wait for an answer.

Squeaky silenced her immediately and gave a few words of blonde wisdom. "Not all of us can be good at everything. Not even being in public."

I looked at Squeaky with complete and utter disillusion. *Being in public—what the hell was that supposed to mean?* I didn't care to ask nor did I care about decrypting the inner workings of a yellow-haired sea-harp. Since it wasn't relevant to my story whatsoever, I shook my head and found the part where I had left off.

"So, anyway, I took the appetizers to their table and set them down without harm. But then I turned and saw a spider on the floor and that's when I had a problem. My screams sent the wig-woman at the other table into hysterics. Apparently her hearing aid was accidentally set on high. When she lurched from her seat, the table joined her. Moments later, so did her hair. Turns out, the fabric from her skirt got stuck to the underside of the table and wherever she went, the table went. Her husband's scotch and soda went vaulting towards him with every other part of the meal in tow. They didn't stay long after that."

"Oh my God—that's terrible! That poor spider!" a woman screamed from the other side of the circle.

I glared at the woman. I couldn't believe that she had missed the point. Before I even had a chance to roll my eyes, she continued.

"Was the spider okay? I love those little things but I just can't go outside, I just can't!"

Squeaky stopped her. "Marcia—this is Gracie's story. You can tell us your story again later." The woman nodded and then fell silent.

"So," I said, "I left the floor for a few moments of down time. My boss wasn't too sure if I was okay to go back in but he allowed me to try with my table's main course."

"Oh God," a voice echoed in the room. I looked up and saw Squeaky shaking her head. She was staring at the floor tiles, now avoiding any eye contact with me. I ignored her remark and started again.

"So, I had two plates, one in each hand. Chicken cacciatore in my left and beef stroganoff in my right."

"Oh Christ . . ." someone else whispered.

Peering at the group, I saw several glances being exchanged. Solemn, pensive glances, devoid of happiness. That said, at least their heads were up. I had their focus, or at least my story did.

"As I carried the plates, my hands wobbled. My medication was wearing off and I was starting to feel a little klutzy."

"A little?" Squeaky said, quietly. "Sorry, Gracie, that was rude. I didn't mean that. Carry on."

I frowned at her and then continued. "The young couple at the table were waiting for me, but not in a good way. Their faces were gaunt; the colour had basically drained from their cheeks. And I'm pretty sure that whatever thoughts of romance they might have had, were completely obliterated when I approached their table." My eyes gazed all around the room. The story I had spent the last few minutes describing was reaching its pinnacle. Soon, it would all be over and I could breathe a sigh of relief knowing that there were others that would side with me and appreciate my plight. I had to finish it.

"Their bodies were trembling as the plates tilted precariously over my fingers. They slid their chairs back from the table, which in all honesty did not help with my confidence level. And that's when it happened."

Gasps were heard throughout the room. "What happened?" one person in the circle asked.

"I know—you dropped the food all over them!" a woman yelled out.

"You brought out the wrong meals . . ." another man shouted.

"I can't take this anymore!" An older woman jumped from her chair and raced out of the room.

"Sheila—come back!" Squeaky called out to her but the woman was gone. "Okay, everyone, just calm down." She did her best to keep the mood peaceful and quiet.

I sat for a moment acknowledging the state of excitement within the group. Were they really here to help me? Or was something else going on. I figured my story was dramatic, but running out on it? That was a little over the top.

I leaned back in my chair and exhaled. "Like I said, my medication was wearing off. So, when I set down the plates . . . I thought . . . the food was alive. Literally. I thought the chicken was clucking and the beef was mooing. With both hands I delved into the dishes to try and free them. That's basically when I went bananas. I threw the food at the young couple and laughed viciously at the remaining customers in the room. I took the plates, stood up on the table and howled at the chandelier. I then threw the plates against the walls and screamed for animal liberation. After that, I don't remember much. Except the prick . . ."

First, there was silence. Then someone asked, "What was the prick all about?"

"It was . . . a . . . um . . . sedative . . . to knock me out . . . so that I wouldn't hurt anyone on the way to the hospital."

Everyone in the room was now quiet.

"After that, I was told to get help. I'm in therapy now which is good, but my therapist says it's important to connect with others. And that's why I'm here. To listen and talk to others who understand me," I smiled at them.

I noticed now that the people on either side of me had moved their chairs even further away. *That's odd*, I thought.

Squeaky cleared her throat, looked around the room at then glanced back at me. "Um, Gracie, that's a very interesting story, but I think it's safe to tell you now . . . that you have the wrong room. In fact, it would be best if you left, since you seem to be scaring everyone here."

I could feel the sudden rush of blood to my face. "Wrong room?" The words jiggled out of my mouth.

"Yes," she smiled. "The support group for 'Those Who Can't Serve' is in the next room down the hall. This is a 'Fear of People' meeting."

TEN

LONDON'S FOG

Not to make it sound like a cliché, but it was a warm summer afternoon when this story really began. I sat in a little room, no bigger than my kitchen, waiting patiently for the results of the surgery. It was an event that I had been expecting, although not so soon. The adoption papers that I had signed only three weeks earlier lay tucked within my purse, a credit to my recent role as a new mother. My hands were jittery and my mind was racing. Had I made the right decision? It was all I could think of as I sat silently, contemplating the outcome of the procedure.

Hope came to me as Dr. Thomas entered the room. Her smile was overwhelming and I could feel the flutter in my heart begin to subside. It was hard for me not to think of her as an angel at that very moment.

"He's going to be just fine, we got it just in time. Now, he's going to be out of the loop for a little while, but if you'd like to come back and take a quick peek," she motioned to the door, "then I can take you back there right now."

Tears now coated my eyes as I nodded in response. "Yes, I need to see him, thank you."

Soggy tissues cupped in my hands, I followed her through the door, down the hallway and into another room lined with several large cages. The first thing I noticed was how sterile the area was. Everything was white, shiny and clean. It gave me a calming feeling and I knew it would be the best place for my boy to heal.

"Here's London," Doctor Thomas said, pointing to one of the cages.

I looked down at the large metal box and smiled. It looked like a small condo. A thick black cushion covered the bottom, and chocolate brown drapes hung along the sides like curtains. Hell, I wanted to be inside of it.

"Go ahead," she said in a gentle voice, "take a look at your baby. He's still sleeping from the anesthetic but I know how much you wanted to see him."

Quietly, I knelt down as I pushed one of the curtains aside. A giant sigh escaped my lips when I saw my bundle of white stretched out on the cushion. I could see his little belly moving rhythmically up and down and for some odd reason it reminded me of a Bob Marley song. He looked so relaxed.

"So, the surgery went well?" I said, looking at his furry little face.

"Yes, he was a trooper."

I saw the bandages that covered his eyes and began to cry. "I'm so sorry little one, but it was for the best."

I couldn't help but cry, the whole situation was incredibly sad. Approximately a month ago, a beautiful white five-month-old Husky had been brought into the local animal shelter. The owner had purchased the puppy from a breeder but soon discovered that there was something wrong with its sight. Unfortunately this person didn't have the finances to pay for any surgery and was unsure of how to care for the animal's condition. But in a way, it was fortunate—for me.

Around the time the puppy was left there, I was dealing with my own pet issues. I had been grieving the loss of my cat Radar, a family pet I had loved and owned for fourteen years. He had succumbed to cancer and I had done the humane thing by putting him down. So, with all the love I could give him, I said goodbye.

A week later, on a stormy Monday afternoon, I was driving past the animal shelter. I guess I was feeling melancholy. It didn't help that I had Karen Carpenter's song, 'Rainy Days and Mondays' stuck in my head. As I slowed my car on the wet road, I thought about my little Radar and how he was probably watching me from up above—atop of a branch somewhere, no doubt. I smiled at the thought of him, chasing the squirrels into the trees until he himself was lost in the leaves.

Something stirred inside of me and that's when I turned the car around on the street. I decided to head back to the shelter. I knew what was inside would probably bring me to tears, but I drove the car there anyway.

As I entered the parking lot, my nerves began to weaken. I sat for the next ten minutes just watching the rain dribble down my windshield. I debated whether I could actually make it through the doors. "You can do this," I told myself over and over again as I looked at my reflection in the rear view mirror.

I opened the door and stepped out into the fresh air to inhale my first breath. I forgot however that it was raining and so I quickly shut the door and ran to the front of the building, hauling my hesitations behind me. The front door was heavy as I pulled it open but I continued on until all of me was inside. My senses kicked into high gear as I immediately recognized the smells around me.

"Hi there," a chirpy young voice came from behind the counter. "What can I help you with?"

Peering over the counter, I smiled. "Sorry, I'm just a little shocked at myself. I can't believe that I actually made it inside. I mean, I just lost a pet recently and . . . I guess I'm here to . . . um . . . well . . . actually I don't know what I'm doing here." Geez, I couldn't believe what I was saying. I felt like a crazy person, babbling on and on to someone I had never met before. But this stranger didn't seem to mind.

"It's okay," she said, her eyes sincere. "We've all lost pets, but that doesn't mean we stop loving them."

I nodded my head. My sadness was returning. I stared at the ground, since that's where my tears were headed anyway. Stupidly, I had left the tissues in the car. But out of the corner of my eye I saw sympathy heading my way, the young woman was handing me a tissue.

Turning away, I blew my nose and dried my eyes. I waited until the moment was right and I was able to face her again. Looking up from the floor, I now saw a board on the wall, covered with animal photos. "Are these all animals that are here right now?" I said, my nose clogged.

"No, those are pets that have been adopted. They're just like family members, so we take pictures of them before they leave so that we'll remember them."

"That's really nice. My cat was from a shelter—his name was Radar," I said, turning back to look at her. "He was my baby and I miss him very much."

The woman gave a knowing smile. "It's hard isn't it?"

"Yes," I said, blowing my nose. "I guess in a weird way, this is therapy."

"Well, would you like to look at some of the animals here?"

My answer was delayed. "Oh boy . . . I don't know. I mean . . . it was hard enough for me to just get through the front door."

"That's understandable," she said. "Would you like it if I went with you?"

I nodded. "Sure, that would be nice."

The woman called over to a co-worker nearby to let her know she was leaving her seat. She then came around the side of the counter and led me down a long corridor.

"Would you like to start with the cats or the dogs?"

"Oh, dogs. I think seeing cats right now would be too hard," I said, following closely behind her.

She then opened a large door and we both walked into a room filled with barking. "These guys actually spend a lot of time outside. We're lucky here—we have the space for them to really move around. They're all in right now because of the rain."

I watched as she moved alongside the cages, speaking tenderly to each and every dog. "Hi guys, how are ya? Hello, Sparky. Hi Jake—how's the paw? And how's my little Muffin?" she said, crouching down by one of the cages.

I giggled internally at the name but when I saw the little Chihuahua staring back at her, I realized that the name seemed very fitting.

"And how are you, pretty boy?" she said, moving on.

I couldn't see the next animal she was speaking to until I walked over and stood next to her. Lying on the floor of the cage, was a white pile of fluff, curled up, looking out the side. He didn't even look back at the woman. "He seems pretty quiet," I said, looking him over.

"Well, this little guy was brought in about a week ago. He has some sort of eye condition and the owner couldn't afford his care."

I stared at the small animal for a few minutes, waiting for him to look over at us, but he never did. His head rested on his paws as he looked out the side of the cage. I walked over to the corner of the enclosure and watched as his little eyebrows moved up and down. His gaze now focused on the ground.

Although the soft spot of my heart was generally reserved for the companionship of felines, I felt immediately drawn to this animal. "What sort of eye condition does he have?"

"I'm not sure, exactly. The vet examined him but the test results won't be in for a couple of days. But I think whatever it is, is degenerative."

What was going on here? This little guy didn't seem to care about anything. His food dish was full, he wasn't eating. He was just staring out into space like a being without any hope. What was happening to him?

What I did know, was that it had taken me all of five minutes in the company of this animal to realize what I wanted to do. "Is he spoken for?"

"No. A family came to see him two days ago but we haven't heard back from them."

"Good," I said. "Because I want him."

The woman looked at me with a surprised expression. "That's the fastest adoption I've ever seen," she laughed.

"Yeah, well, I'm a little surprised myself, actually. But I want him. What do I need to sign?"

Now, post-op, I sat looking in at my puppy as he lay sprawled out on the cushion. Thank God he was okay. With the success of the surgery came my relief. I was not going to be comfortable doing anything until I knew the outcome. That's why I remained at the clinic during the surgery. And boy was I worried. I had never had a pet with a serious affliction at such a young age. Although cancer took Radar's life, it was not until the end of his days.

But this little guy here was only six months old. And the surgery was necessary for his survival. The cancer that had grown quickly in the last few weeks had taken away most of his sight. The only way to remedy the situation was to have both eyes removed. It was a subject matter that I had difficulty understanding, for if it were me, I don't know if I would have responded well to the idea of surgery.

The decision was made in the best interest of the animal. He would have the surgery, and for the rest of his years he would see life without sight.

Looking down at him, I smiled. "Oh, my sweet London, we're going to have such a wonderful life together, just you and me."

A soft grunt came from his mouth as if he understood.

Dr. Thomas then opened the door to the room. I pulled the curtain around the front of the cage and pressed my hand against it. "Soon you'll be home and we can begin our new life together." I then stood and walked out the door.

* * *

The day had come. I was awake at an early hour—my excitement was paving the way for the day's events. London was coming home. After an hour of preparation, I was on my way to the veterinary clinic to pick up my boy. The house was loaded with toys, gates, food and bones. I wanted to make sure that London really felt that he was taken care of and spoiled rotten. After all that he had been through, I figured indulging him was absolutely necessary.

I drove to the clinic, hands clenched around the wheel as my heart raced towards the parking lot. Once I arrived, I jumped out of the vehicle covered in giddiness and made my way to the front door. As I entered, I felt a weird sensation encompass me. It was a strange sort of happiness mixed with anxiety. How would London feel coming home? Would he be happy? Would he want to be with me? These questions were about to be answered.

Dr. Thomas entered the waiting room with the cage in her hand. "He's getting heavier," she laughed. "He's been eating non-stop the last few days here."

"So I've heard. I have lots of food for him at home."

"I'll take him to your car," she said, "if you could just open the doors."

"Of course," I scurried towards the door.

Once he was positioned in the car, I let out a giant sigh. The time had come. London was finally coming home.

As I opened the front door of the house, I heard a noise come from inside the cage. It was London, and he seemed excited. It didn't hit me until we entered the house: he knew we were home. It was amazing. Not only had he lived here less than a month, but he no longer had his sight to visualize his surroundings. But he knew where he was. It was my first indication that things were going to be all right.

I closed the door behind me as I rested the cage on the floor. Slowly, I opened the metal door. I figured that after an operation like that, he would want to take his time moving around the house. Could I have been more wrong? London lurched out of the cage and quickly made his way down the hallway towards the kitchen. That's where the food and water was. I watched in amazement at he reached down to the bowls on the floor. He was nimble and athletic. Then it occurred to me that he hadn't much eyesight before the surgery anyway. And in the last three weeks of living here, he had become accustomed to his surroundings with hardly any sight. So, right now, things were somewhat normal. The only difference being the little crosses that now held his eyelids closed.

I walked into the kitchen and sat on the floor beside him. Gently, I patted his soft white coat as he polished off the remaining kibble in the dish. "That's a good London," I said, hoping he would remember my voice. He then turned around and licked me on the nose. Wow, I thought. He knew exactly where my face was. Although his sight was now gone, his other senses were very acute. I just sat there in awe of him.

London then walked onto my legs and nudged me with his nose. He wanted me to continue petting him. As I lifted my hand to touch his furry torso, he placed himself beneath my fingers as if to help guide them. I laughed. "Say, who had the surgery here?" He then moved all four feet onto my legs and curled up on my lap. He was preparing for a nap.

It was then that I realized—London had triumphed over his disability. He wasn't defeated, he was a victorious fighter with a heart full of strength. All he needed was a chance to show it.

I've learned many things from London. I consider him one of my greatest teachers. But the one thing that stands out in my mind was his perseverance. He taught me never to give up. He showed me that although life can sometimes be crippling, it doesn't have to stop us. If anything, it makes us better, stronger.

For me, it took a friend like London to prove it.

ELEVEN

A FATHER'S FLIGHT

He was only nineteen years old when he turned his back and left home. The U.S. Navy was calling to him, with a future bright and promising. He wasn't in a rush to get there, he was only in a hurry to leave.

I knew the story well. It was about my father's search for happiness as a young man. It started when he was five, when he saw his first airplane in the sky. "That's what I'm going to do," he told himself. He knew it from the moment he looked up at the plane.

That's the story I was told. And as I grew, I began to understand it more and more.

I was the daughter of a Pilot and boy was I proud. My father knew exactly what he wanted to do when he was young and he let nothing stand in his way. To me, it was amazing. He was a man with a dream and the passion to chase it. Up and away he soared, to a sky so blue it was limitless. His wings allowed him the freedom that his chains on earth would not. And in the sky he found happiness.

As a boy, he sought out the runway and as a teen he raced towards it. Hours were logged at the St. Catharines airport where he spent all his spare time learning how to fly. Then suddenly, his feet were brought back to earth when his mother, Bianca, fell ill.

Bianca had been sick before but she had fought her way back and regained her strength. They discovered cancer had grown inside of her, leaving its symptomatic traces within her system. She was taken in for surgery to have a breast removed, which alleviated the worry but not the pain. It appeared that the cancer had been stopped. And life for Bianca began again.

My father's thoughts returned to flying while life at home continued on as normal. But day by day Bianca grew weary as something once again grew inside of her. Her husband was lost at times, not knowing why she was ailing. My father didn't quite know what was happening, not all the information had been disclosed to him. Cancer in the 1950's was still primordial. No one would talk about it.

They soon discovered that Bianca's surgery hadn't stopped the disease. The cancer had spread. I remember one story my father told me about her. He described her as a determined woman, a fighter, a victor, which made this particular story much more disturbing. He said that she had tried to make him breakfast one day but was sickened by the sight of the eggs in the frying pan. She collapsed onto the floor. My father was terrified, horrified by his mother's weakened state.

How my grandmother's disease progressed after that, I don't know. My father wouldn't talk about it. I gathered some information from my aunt and some from my own mother who had never met her mother-in-law but had heard stories herself. For the most part, it was like Bianca had just disappeared. All that was left was a slab of granite that my father visited frequently.

Everything else I was told about my grandmother occurred before the cancer. My father showed me pictures of when she was young, unmarried, with friends and some from when she started dating my grandfather. The carefree times. But even that was hard for my father to talk about. It seemed that every time I brought up her name, he'd stop talking. He was despondent. There were even times when I asked about my grandmother he would say, "She wasn't your grandmother—you never met her." His own words seemed to upset him though, and I wondered why he would distance his family from her. I couldn't understand it.

I do know that after Bianca died, my father shut down. It was quite clear to me. No one ever said it, but I knew that's what must have happened. His life had changed. He lost his most beloved friend in the world. It was the one person who believed in him and knew he was capable of many great things. How could his loss ever be understood? That's when he decided to leave.

He turned to the U.S. Navy and went through training as an Interior Communications Electronics Technician. From the USS Valley Forge to the USS Boxer, he trained and worked.

And then in 1961 he became the first crew to board the aircraft carrier, USS Kitty Hawk in Philadelphia. With that, he left behind his loss, his anger and his pain. He shut down his old life and began a new one.

After his years in the Navy, my father returned home to Canada. He lived with his father in a house coated with nothing but tension and memories. It didn't take him long to leave. This time he was off to the Canadian Air Force in Gimli, Manitoba, to do exactly what he wanted to do—fly. From trainee to pilot, from training officer to Captain—he rose in the ranks like a starling lifting its wings. Off he went to a life most coveted and from there he found true bliss.

His life in the sky brought a strong career to build a family on. My brother was born in Chandler, Arizona, when my father worked as a training officer for the U.S. Air Force. When I arrived on the scene, my family had just moved to Montreal from Bagotville, where my father flew with a fighter squadron. He was leaving the Air Force to become a commercial airline pilot.

As my parents travelled from job to job, they found themselves collecting many objects of value, the most important being the family pets. Odin, our German shepherd was their first collectible. Toby, our Siamese cat was the second. Both pets were adopted into the family before my brother and I were even born. Toby was my father's first Valentine's gift to my mom. Odin, was my father's first headache. Regardless, those beautiful animals brought my parents undeniable joy and company. And laughter, too.

The animals that ruled our roost however were the cats. The Siamese cats. Growing up, we always had one . . . or two . . . or three . . . or four. I guess you could say our family was biased. It started with Toby, then Tash, then Ming and Bailey. And then came Jasmine.

Jasmine was my cat, we adopted each other. I was twenty-five and living at home, and she was seven weeks old and utterly adorable. We aged together; everywhere I went, she went. And her favourite way to travel was via my neck. Every time my neck was bare, she would wrap herself around my shoulders like a warm scarf. A cuddly, squishy, Seal point scarf. God, she was amazing. She was athletic, nimble, calculating and brilliant.

Every so often we would let her outside to smell the backyard grass. And within seconds, she'd be gone. She would scale the garage and jump onto the neighbour's roof. We would get panicked phone calls from those next door saying how they spotted our Jasmine outside their window. Boy, she was a talented one. But as quickly as she would disappear, she would reappear. She would saunter back into the yard and whine at the door to be let in. I soon realized that she was just like that beautiful Siamese from

'That Darn Cat'. Jasmine had her route and it was all planned out. So why worry?

For an indoor cat, she intrigued us. Her behaviour was almost human. When she looked at you, you just knew that she wanted to say something. I guess that's partly why her death was so saddening. It was as if there was a little person in there. My best friend had left me.

When Jasmine was seven, she was diagnosed with a brain tumour. It pressed on her optic nerves, leaving her completely blind. Little coats of fog covered both of her eyes. It broke my heart just looking at her. This vibrant, fearless animal had been struck down by cancer. And it devastated our family.

Although she was my girl, my father took it the hardest. He was absolutely silent. His heart bled for Jasmine and I saw a side of him that I had never seen before. He wept at the sight of her little body as week by week it dwindled down to nothing. But still he wouldn't talk about his feelings. He remained sealed amongst his memories.

On the day we took Jasmine to the vet, we couldn't contain ourselves. Our grief, our anguish was uncontrollable. This amazing animal had touched us all. One by one, we said our goodbyes as we hugged her and laid her down. Slowly, her spirit left her body as she gently drifted off to another place. A place where we all hoped to meet again. Sobbing was all anyone could hear. The room was filled with our tears and sadness.

We decided to bury her at home. But before we could take her there, there was one last place she needed to see. It was completely unexpected as my father was the only one who knew where we were going. He drove the car in silence as my mother, brother and I wondered about the direction we were headed in. Jasmine lay on my lap, wrapped in a mohair blanket. All her pain was gone. She was at peace.

It wasn't until we entered the cemetery that I understood what was about to happen. My father parked the car alongside the row of headstones and opened the door. "Hand her to me, Kara," he said with watery eyes. Carefully, I placed Jasmine into his arms as he began to walk among the gravestones. He stopped when he came upon the one he desired. "Mom—I'm here now. I've brought you someone to look after. Here she is," he cried. "You need to take care of her now. Please, take care of her!"

Behind him we all stood, now understanding the source of his grief. It was Bianca who had led him to the cemetery, the woman he had never grieved for. But here he was, mourning her loss through the death of this animal. And from Jasmine's death, came a light that burned inside of him, one the rest of us had never seen. He finally accepted his mother's death; he allowed it to wash over him. And at that moment we knew that his heart had opened up. The healing process had begun.

Days after we buried Jasmine, my father began to speak. He talked about our grandmother. He allowed her to touch us through his stories. Dad told us that she was a champion, someone who stood up for others and spoke her mind about issues. Our grandmother was a tough, hard-working lady with love for everyone and everything. I could see why she was my father's hero.

It was then that I truly understood the meaning of it all. The day he broke was the day he began to heal. I saw my father in his entirety and it felt peaceful for the first time.

In essence, his wings had allowed him to touch the sky but it was the love of our Jasmine that allowed him to walk again.

ABOUT THE AUTHOR

Kara Bartley has always been interested in animals, so it comes as no surprise that her world is surrounded by them in both her life and imagination.

She has a bachelor's degree in Biology/Earth Science, a post-graduate diploma in Geographic Information Systems and a master's degree in Vertebrate Paleontology. In the spring of 2002, she began writing her first novel, *The Siamese Mummy,* while on a dig for fossils in Kansas.

Kara is also the author of *The Unearthlings, Call of Adhara* and *The Moon In Habock's Mirror*. She lives in Niagara Falls, Ontario, with her three Siamese cats Apollo, Achilles and Agamemnon. Her horse, Dapplynn, is her biggest companion and anxiously awaits the day that she too, will have a guest appearance in one of her mother's books.

ABOUT THE ILLUSTRATOR

Tammy Dunlavey grew up in North East, Pennsylvania with the innate ability to draw. When it came to education, Tammy chose science over art, as science offered her a path untaken.

In August of 2001, Tammy was diagnosed with Multiple sclerosis. In light of her medical challenges, she continued on and graduated with a master's degree in Invertebrate Paleontology.

Although Tammy has returned to her artistic roots, she finds that paleontology often appears within her art. Her journey with MS has also played a significant role in her work as her health experiences are well expressed in her creativity.

She is inspired by her son, Keegan, her daughter, Ellen, her granddaughter, Molly-Jane, her husband, Brent and her parents. Tammy's extended family of four-legged pets also provide her with much love and amusement.

THE PALEO TWINS

Tammy and I first met at grad school in the fall of 2002. The first thing I remember her saying was, "Oh—*she* must be the Vertebrate Palaeontologist!" From that moment on, we were friends.

We shared an office in the geology department at the University at Buffalo where Tammy studied Invertebrate Paleontology and I studied Vertebrate Paleontology. Two rival scientists with a common love of fossils and animal history. Who would have known?

Throughout our studies, we talked and travelled. At school we were given the name, 'The Paleo Twins,' and to our delight, it stuck. Tammy became my sister and for the years we spent in that office, I felt like I had family.

I soon found out that my twin had an amazing flare for artistry, whereas I began to succumb to the creativeness of words. Two scientists turned artists, I'm sure our professors are still scratching their heads.

It was through school that we met as friends but it was paleontology that brought us together as artists. Our support for one another transcended our education as Tammy and I joined forces once again for my novels. She is the illustrator behind the words and I am the storyteller behind the pictures.

Hopefully this will not be our last creative endeavour!

CPSIA information can be obtained at www.ICGtesting.com
Printed in the USA
LVOW122220180413
329662LV00001B/17/P

9 781483 620213